RYAN'S RESCUE©

Diana I. Kline

Copyright © by Diana I. Kline
All right reserved.

Published by the Columbus Historical Society

Columbus, Ohio

ISBN: 978-1-964747-02-6

Dedication

This story is dedicated to Fran Ryan, life-long Columbus, Ohio resident and long-standing contributor to our city. Fran's commitment to the Columbus Historical Society Engine House No. 6 project made this book possible.

Table of Contents

Foreword 4
Chapter 1. Ryan 7
Chapter 2. Benjamin and Ellie 13
Chapter 3. Ryan's First Visit 16
Chapter 4. The Successful Shopping Trip 21
Chapter 5. Lost and Found 27
Chapter 6. A Possible Link 31
Chapter 7. Fire Station No. 10 35
Chapter 8. Making the History Connection 41
Chapter 9. Lots of Changes 45
Chapter 10. Ryan's Rescue 51
About the Author and Illustrator 53
Endnotes 57

Foreword

As a board member for the Columbus Historical Society (CHS), I have had the privilege of meeting many local individuals who have given so much of their time and talents to Columbus. It has been stimulating to hear from various Columbus groups about their needs and desires and how the CHS might help them reach their goals.

CHS is often asked to help instruct area youth about the history of Franklinton and Columbus. I discussed this interest with board member Fran Ryan and suggested that creating a children's book could help accomplish this. "Ryan," our ceramic Dalmatian, who is moving from the temporary Town Street CHS office to Engine House No. 6, our new permanent headquarters in Franklinton, seemed like the perfect model for the main character.

I saw Diana Kline's book, *A Solar System Chat*, at a local shipping store, *Ship Print eSell*, where the store's owners, Jason Hartwig and Matt Resatar, graciously display books written by local authors. After reading and sharing Diana's book with others, she offered to write the story and her book's illustrator, Suzy Cornetet, volunteered to create the images.

Ryan's Rescue is a story about Ryan and how he learns that change may be difficult yet may result in a positive outcome. He receives help on his journey from his friends, co-workers, and total strangers, and they learn a bit of Columbus history along the way. "Real-life" themes are included, such as moving from place to place and the emotional challenges that may result, the joys and responsibilities of pet ownership, the enjoyment and privilege of life-long learning, and the human connection that helps all of us through life's changes and challenges.

Luna

The story should be a reminder to all of us that if you are seven years old or seventy, you can work through tough times in your life with the support of your family, your friends, and even total strangers by taking one step at a time.

And finally, I would like to thank Luna for her "real-life" paw print. We appreciate her willingness to lend us a "paw."

Jody Maclean
Secretary / Chair of Member Services
Columbus Historical Society

Chapter 1. Ryan

"Hmm…I wonder what's going on?" thought Ryan, the big Dalmatian, as he looked around at all the boxes. Boxes were everywhere: cardboard boxes, plastic boxes, and metal boxes. Some were big, some were small, and some were in-between. He slid down, put his head between his paws, and just stared up at all of them. So many boxes and so much disruption. And, there are not many visitors here lately.

"I love this place, but I don't like all this confusion," thought Ryan.

Anne, the Columbus Historical Society assistant director, saw Ryan looking sad in the corner surrounded by all the chaos and clutter. Although Anne loves her usual role of greeting visitors and giving tours of the exhibits to families and school groups, her main job these days is helping the Society pack and move from its current home at 717 West Town Street to a new one a few blocks away at 540 West Broad Street. She wondered if he could be upset about this big move.

"Ryan, you will love visiting the new home of the Columbus Historical Society! You will have so much fun when you come with me to work. You have enjoyed coming here to visit, so I think you will like the new place even better!" said Anne.

RYAN'S RESCUE

Ryan just looked up at Anne and stared with his big, gloomy eyes. "I don't think so," thought Ryan. "I love it here on Town Street! I don't want to move!" He sunk down even further onto the floor.

Just then Benjamin, Ellie, and their mom, Jane Simpson, walked in. The Simpson family had often visited here before. Ryan perked up and barked a big hello. He was so happy to see their friendly faces!

Benjamin and Ellie saw Ryan in the corner and heard his loud barks. They ran over to him and gave him many pets and big hugs.

Anne was thrilled to see the visitors as well. "Hello! I see it's the Simpson family – back for another visit! I remember your family has come here many times to see our exhibits and take part in our programs on the history of Columbus. And, look at Ryan! He is thrilled to see you!"

"We love coming here!" said Mrs. Simpson. "We have learned so much from all your interesting exhibits, not to mention the fun time we had at the outdoor concert you hosted. And because I've come here on field trips as a teacher, I'd have to say that my students and I have learned a lot about Columbus history here."

"What's up with all the boxes?" Benjamin asked while he and Ellie petted Ryan.

Anne smiled. "We're moving! We're packing up and getting ready for the movers to come next week. Our new home will be on West Broad Street, not too far from here. This was our temporary space until the Society purchased a new permanent site."

"Oh, that's exciting!" said Mrs. Simpson. "We came in because Benjamin has a school project on the history of transportation. I thought you might have some information or photos on early automobiles."

"You're right!" said Anne. "I was just packing up some photos and newspaper articles on two antique automobiles that the society has acquired recently. The cars are over 100 years old and will be part of our first exhibit in our new museum. You might be interested in seeing these photos."

"These pictures are so cool!" said Benjamin. "I have never seen old cars like this!"

Anne also showed them an old photo of a horse-drawn buggy before cars that ran on gasoline. "Wow," said Benjamin. "That buggy is *really* old!"

"Yes, it is," said Anne. "That photo is from the Columbus Buggy Works, back when Columbus was known as 'the buggy capital of the world.' If you want me to, Benjamin, I could make copies of these pictures and other information for your school project. This will show the transition in transportation from horse-drawn vehicles to motorized vehicles in the early years of the 20th century."

"That would be awesome, Anne! Thank you so much!" said Benjamin.

"So, you're moving not far from here, Anne?" asked Mrs. Simpson. "We will definitely want to visit often. We always learn so much when we stop by."

"We are moving to an older building on West Broad Street that has been boarded up for many years. The Society acquired it, and now it is being restored. It will be a beautiful place and a perfect home for us," said Anne.

"Interesting!" said Mrs. Simpson. "That is close to where we live. In fact, I think I know which building you are talking about. It has been boarded up for quite a while, hasn't it?"

"Yes, it has been," said Anne. "But now it's being renovated and it's looking beautiful! Instead of tearing the building down to build something new, we wanted to save the old building since it is part of Columbus' history."

"What a great idea!" said Mrs. Simpson. "Will Ryan get to visit there just like he does here?"

"Yes, Ryan will continue to come to work with me occasionally. We will be on the first floor with the exhibits while the work continues on the rest of the building. As you know, he loves to be here with me and see all the people coming in. He gets lots of attention that way," said Anne as she watched him smiling and wagging his tail in the corner with Benjamin and Ellie. "He has really missed seeing people since we announced that we are moving. And, he has not gotten out for a walk today because I am so busy packing up all our materials and supplies!"

Ellie got excited, since she loves dogs. "We would love to take Ryan out for a walk! Can we do that, Mom?"

"You can take him for a walk if it's OK with Anne," said Mrs. Simpson. "Maybe Anne would let us take Ryan to his new neighborhood so he can check it out? And, then we will know where the Columbus Historical Society's new home will be. What do you think, Anne? We can bring Ryan back in an hour or so."

Anne smiled and said, "Ryan would love that! That would give Ryan a chance to visit his new neighborhood. Maybe that will make him feel better about this move. Let me get his leash."

RYAN'S RESCUE

Chapter 2. Benjamin and Ellie

Once Benjamin and Ellie got to Mom's car, Ryan hopped in the back seat, and Ellie jumped in beside him. After they all buckled their seat belts, Mrs. Simpson headed toward West Broad Street. Benjamin and Ellie loved having Ryan in the car with them. And, Ryan was so happy with the wind in his face and the sights and sounds whizzing by.

Ellie wondered as she watched Ryan. "Mom, do you think we could ever get a dog? I really like Ryan."

"That's a possibility, Ellie. I know you and Benjamin enjoy seeing Ryan when we visit the Columbus Historical Society. And, as you can tell, he loves being with you! We came to Columbus so your father could go back to school and earn a master's degree, so, when he is finished, we may move again — just like Ryan is moving now. Maybe if we move, we can get a dog. We'll see."

Once they got home, Ryan jumped out of the car, and Ellie held on tightly to his leash.

Mom saw how happy they were, even Ryan! "Ellie and Benjamin, please walk Ryan down past the old building that will be the Columbus Historical Society's new home."

"OK, Mom," said Benjamin, "I just need to eat something first – I'm hungry." He poured himself a glass of milk and peeled a banana. Ellie filled a bowl with water for Ryan, and he slurped it up quickly.

"Also, Mom, can we go to the sports store today?" said Benjamin.

"Why, Benjamin? As I recall, shopping is **not** one of your favorite things to do," said Mom with a smile.

"I want this new soccer ball that my friend, Jayden, was telling me about."

"Oh, Benjamin. You and soccer! I know how much you love that game! Maybe someday, you will be playing for the Columbus Crew!"

"Please take Ryan for a walk. Then, after we take him back to the historical society, maybe we can go shopping. I need some paper for our printer. We're out," replied Mom.

Benjamin sighed. "Can't Ryan just hang out here with us?"

"No. Benjamin, he needs a walk now. Ellie just asked if we could have a dog someday. Having a pet means taking on responsibilities that you sometimes don't want to do. And, you saw how sad he was today at the building on Town Street. I'm not sure why. I don't think he wants to leave there. You don't have to take him very far — just near the new site of the historical society."

Benjamin looked out the kitchen window. "It's kind of rainy now, Mom," said Benjamin.

Mom gave Benjamin a bit of a stare and chuckled. "Take the umbrella, Benjamin. It's in the closet. After you and Ellie take him for a walk, then we will discuss a shopping trip. And, who knows, maybe the sun will be shining when we get back home, and you and Jayden can play soccer!"

Chapter 3. Ryan's First Visit

Benjamin and Ellie started down the street, and Ryan was pulling *them*! He loved all the different buildings he had never seen before and all the new smells! Soon, they were in front of the old, brick building that had been boarded up for several years.

Suddenly, they all stopped and stared at the old building that they had seen before.

Benjamin and Ellie couldn't believe what they saw. As they looked at it, they were seeing all kinds of craftspeople – carpenters, electricians, plumbers, painters, and others – going in and out the door. These workers were using their skills and talents to bring this old building back to life. "It used to look so deserted but look at it now!" said Benjamin. "I can't wait to go inside to see what it looks like."

"Wow!" agreed Ellie. "This place is looking totally different. I think Ryan will love it here. I'm just curious what this building was – was it somebody's house?"

"I never noticed this building much until now," said Benjamin, but, look at those two large front doors. And, see? One door says 'ENGINE' above it, and the other one says, 'HOSE REEL.' Those big, wide doors must have been where something large had to get into and out of the building -- like the garage doors on a house."

"And, look! See those letters on that stone block above the doors?" noticed Benjamin. "It says 'ENGINE HOUSE NO. 6.' So, it must have been a *fire station!*"

"You're right!" said Ellie. "But I don't think we should get too close. We don't want to get in the way of the workers. We will be able to come here a lot once the Columbus Historical Society moves in and all the exhibits are set up."

Clearly, Ryan wanted to get closer. Ryan started pulling Ellie toward the fire station. "I don't think we can get in it, Benjamin, but we can walk around it, don't you think? Look at Ryan -- *he* seems interested in it – he's doing a lot of sniffing. Let's check it out."

"OK," said Benjamin. "But let's not stay too long. I want to get to the sports store."

Ryan kept pulling on his leash. Ellie struggled to keep Ryan from rushing ahead. He was pulling them toward the back of the building.

Once they all got to the backyard, Ryan started barking a lot and pawing at the ground.

"I wonder if he smells animals around this old building, like animals that lived here in the past?" said Benjamin.

Suddenly, Ryan started digging and pawing at the loose, soft dirt. He wasn't stopping, it seemed.

Finally, after lots of panting, barking, and digging, Ryan pulled out an old piece of leather with a rusty metal buckle attached. It looked like an old animal collar.

He put it in his mouth and would not let it go. Both Ellie and Benjamin tried to get that old piece of leather out of Ryan's mouth, but Ryan held on tight.

"Let's just let him have it and let him carry it back home," said Ellie.

"I guess that's alright," agreed Benjamin as they started walking back toward home. "Ryan is not going to let go of it, that's for sure!"

Back at the Town Street building, Ryan was excited and still carrying what looked like an old collar in his mouth. Anne noticed that he didn't want to let it go or lose sight of it. He had lots of toys in his toy box on Town Street, but this old piece of leather was now his favorite.

Anne wondered about his change of behavior. She thought Ryan seemed happier and more relaxed. "I wonder why he is carrying that old piece of leather in his mouth? I know he may not want to leave this building, but he does seem better since he went for a walk. Maybe he just needed some fresh air and exercise," thought Anne.

But Ryan knew he was happy about something else. "I *really* like this old collar," he thought. "It smells like *me*! I want to hold on to it. I wonder when I can get back to that old building again?!?"

He settled down in his soft doggy bed with his "old, new" collar by his side and took a much-needed nap.

RYAN'S RESCUE

Chapter 4. The Successful Shopping Trip

At the sports store, Benjamin found the soccer ball that he wanted. Mom got her paper for the printer at the office supply store. And Ellie got to stop in the nearby bookstore and found a book about dogs. Ellie really loved seeing Ryan at the Columbus Historical Society earlier today and taking him for a walk. She hoped that someday she could have a dog of her own like him. She didn't know a lot about Ryan except that he has lots of black spots all over his large, white-fur body.

At the dinner table that night, Benjamin talked about his new soccer ball and playing with Jayden in the backyard. The sun did come out, and they got to practice for their team's soccer game this weekend.

Then Ellie piped up as well. "Mom and Dad, I love my new book. I am learning about all kinds of dogs. Did you know that Ryan is called a 'Dalmatian'?"

"Yes, we knew that, Ellie. Your mother and I have seen Ryan at the Columbus Historical Society when we have visited there," said Dad. "Did you read what Dalmatians are used for?"

"Hmm," said Ellie. "No, but I'll keep reading to find out."

As she was reading between her delicious bites of pot roast and her apple crisp dessert, she found the chapter about Dalmatians.

"Dad, did you know that Dalmatians often lived at fire stations?"

Dad smiled as he sat down his coffee cup. "Yes, Ellie, I knew that. But I really don't know *why* Ryan's type of dog lived at fire stations. What does your book say about that? Is it because of their strong sense of smell? That's what I would think.'"

Ellie kept reading. "No, it's not that, Dad. That's what I was thinking, too. It's because of their strong bond with horses and their ability to run long distances."[1]

"But Ellie, there are no horses at the fire stations," said Dad. "That doesn't make sense."

Ellie rolled her eyes and smiled. "In the old days, horses pulled the fire engines. Remember, there were no fire trucks years ago. In fact, this morning at the Columbus Historical Society, Anne showed us photos of old horse-drawn buggies that were actually built in Columbus before gasoline-powered cars were invented."

"Wow – that *is* interesting, Ellie! Even I learned something today!"

Benjamin piped up. "Dad, I thought *you* knew everything!"

"No, believe it or not, I don't know everything, Benjamin," said Dad with a smile. "We are always learning."

Ellie kept reading. "Before firehouses, Dalmatians were bred and trained to prevent highway robbery of stagecoaches! They would run beside the horse-drawn stagecoaches and act as buffers and bodyguards for the stagecoach occupants!

"My book says, 'in the US the Dalmatian was used as a 'firehouse dog,' running with horse-drawn fire engines and clearing the way for them. Some fire stations still keep Dalmatians as mascots.' "[2]

Ellie continued, "They were probably a great choice with their bright, white coats and large black spots, since they were so visible.

"When we discussed pets at school recently, our teacher mentioned that certain dog breeds may be deaf due to a genetic condition, and I think Dalmatians are one of these breeds.[3] This trait would probably be helpful to Dalmatians with the loud fire engine sirens nearby. But it could cause injuries if they do not hear passing cars in the roadways."

Now, it was Mom's turn to smile. "My goodness, all that information is so interesting! I never knew those facts about Dalmatians. I guess I learned something today, too!"

Benjamin laughed. "Mom, I thought you knew everything, for sure! You and Dad seem so smart!"

Mom sighed, "No, Benjamin. Even *we* are always learning – just because we are your parents doesn't mean we know *everything!* As you know, your dad came to Columbus for its excellent schools of higher learning. He's getting his master's degree so he can learn even more valuable knowledge and skills."

Dad agreed, "Your mother's right – we don't know everything, and if we did, life might get a bit boring, don't you think?"

Benjamin wasn't so sure. "Maybe," said Benjamin. "But I sure would like to know everything that is going to be on my math test tomorrow!"

"Well, be sure to study tonight, Benjamin," said Dad. "That will help!

"In fact, I need to study tonight for an exam tomorrow as well, Benjamin. After we help your mom clean up the kitchen from dinner, we can both study here at the kitchen table. Deal?"

Benjamin smiled. "Deal!"

Chapter 5. Lost and Found

The next day at work, Anne noticed that Ryan continued to keep the collar that he found yesterday close to him. He would often pick it up and walk around with it in his mouth.

Anne wondered why. She asked her co-worker, Barb, for her opinion. "Well, you know that dogs have a powerful sense of smell. Maybe the collar has a smell that Ryan likes, or it reminds him of something," said Barb.

Anne agreed. "You're right, Barb. I wonder if we could check out that old collar somehow? I wonder where Ryan found it. I think I'll call Mrs. Simpson and ask her."

When Ellie got home from school, she went to the kitchen for a snack. Mom was standing at the stove stirring the chili for dinner. Ellie was still thinking about Ryan. "Why do you think Ryan was sniffing so much yesterday on his walk, Mom? He seemed like he couldn't sniff enough! And, he was so excited to pull that old piece of leather out of the ground!"

Mom smiled. "Well, Ellie, remember Anne from the Columbus Historical Society? She called me today and left a voice message. Anne wanted to know more about that old piece of leather because Ryan has not let go of it since he got back to the Town Street historical society building yesterday. My guess is he must have smelled something that he liked — or didn't like — something that made him curious. Just like we are always learning, Ryan learns by sniffing!"

"That's interesting, Mom. My book says that Dalmatians have a very strong sense of smell, so something set him off, for sure!" said Ellie.

"Where did he find it, Ellie? Along the sidewalk as you were walking yesterday?" asked Mom.

"No, he found it in the backyard of the old firehouse where the historical society will be moving," said Ellie.

Just then, Benjamin walked into the kitchen, opened the refrigerator door, and pulled out the milk carton. "Wow, that building is looking so cool," he said. "There were a lot of workers there yesterday fixing it up. I didn't want to get too close, but Ellie wanted to and so did Ryan! He kept pulling Ellie along on the leash."

"Hmm…." said Mom. "I wonder why."

"He was so excited to be digging in the ground behind that fire station," said Benjamin. "It seemed like he was really trying to get something and when he pulled out that old piece of leather that looked like a collar, Ellie and I were really surprised!"

Mom continued, "Benjamin, I just told Ellie that Anne called me today. According to her, Ryan carried that old piece of leather around with him all day yesterday when he got back and all day today. He is even *sleeping* with it. He won't let it go. It's kind of strange, really. Anne said he has all his other toys nearby, but he keeps holding on to that piece of leather. Now, my curiosity is up!"

"I wonder what kind of collar it was?" said Ellie. "Do you think we could find out? Maybe it was a farm animal or something from the past – like an animal that used to live near there. Maybe there were farms in that area."

"It's probably just an old animal collar," said Benjamin as he drank his glass of milk and munched on some grapes.

"Well, now that you mentioned it – maybe we could check the library and see what old animal collars looked like? They may have a book about different types of animal collars and leashes. They may know what animal would use that type of collar."

RYAN'S RESCUE

Chapter 6. A Possible Link

Dad was curious about Ryan's find, too, and he agreed with Mom's idea to visit the library. First, Mom stopped back at the Town Street building the next day after work. Anne also thought a visit to the library was in order, so Mom took some photos of the old piece of leather that Ryan had found and headed to the library.

"Guess what, guys?!" said Mom after her visit to the library. "Interesting news today! That piece of leather that Ryan won't let go of is probably an old *dog* collar! And, based on the size and type of leather that he found and the old photos of collars that we found in our research today, the librarian said it was probably a dog collar from about 100 years ago! In fact, the librarian also told me that there are collectors of dog collars – just like there are baseball card and stamp collectors. And, we even found a book about antique dog collars and leashes going back to ancient times![4]

"We could probably find out more information if we keep searching."

Ellie's mind was whirling. "Wow – this *is* interesting. Do you think he *senses* that it is a dog collar? Maybe he feels some kind of connection to it."

Benjamin smiled. "I think you could be onto something, Ellie. He didn't want to let go of it once he found it."

Ellie wondered. "I wonder where Anne got Ryan, Mom. Can you call Anne tomorrow and ask her?"

"Sure," said Mom. "I wonder where this search will lead us now!"

The next night at dinner, they got the latest update on Ryan.

"According to Anne, she got Ryan at the animal shelter — Ryan is a rescue," said Mom.

"Maybe we could check with the animal shelter to see if they know where Ryan came from," said Ellie.

Mom smiled. "You really *are* curious, aren't you, Ellie? And, do you know what? Now, I am too! We will go there tomorrow after school and see what we can find out."

The next day, Mom and Ellie talked with staff members at the animal shelter. They provided some history on Ryan. They remembered that Ryan came from one of the firefighters who worked Fire Station No. 10 [5] at 1096 West Broad Street. Mom knew that Station 10 was not very far from Engine House No. 6 at 540 West Broad where Ryan found the old dog collar. The records at the shelter showed that Ryan was only at the shelter for a few days when he was adopted by their friend Anne who works at the Columbus Historical Society.

"I wonder if the people who work at Station No. 10 know more about Ryan," said Ellie.

"Well, since we are on this scavenger hunt, we shouldn't stop now, right?" said Mom. "Let's go ask them. Maybe they have some more interesting history for us to learn!"

Chapter 7. Fire Station No. 10

When they arrived at Fire Station No. 10, Ellie and her mom could not believe what they saw! The building had an old part attached to a new part. Outside, the old part was beautiful, and it looked a lot like the fire station building down the street from them, but it had been completely restored.

Ellie and her mom went inside. "What a beautiful old building this is!" said Ellie's Mom. "Hi, I am Jane Simpson, and this is my daughter, Ellie."

The firefighter smiled. "Hello, I'm Keith Berwick, one of the firefighters here. Yes, we are very proud of our old building. It was built in 1897, and although the city built a newer addition to accommodate larger modern fire trucks, we still use the old building and are glad they didn't tear it down."

"What did it look like before now?" asked Ellie.

Mr. Berwick walked over to a wall of photos. "Well, let me show you a picture of it before it was restored. It looked like this."

Ellie and her mom followed him over to the photos. When they saw the picture, they smiled. "Yes, that picture looks like the building down the street from our house," said Ellie.

"What building is that?" asked Mr. Berwick.

"It's the building on West Broad Street near Gift Street," said Jane. "It is being restored and will be the new home of the Columbus Historical Society."

"Well," said Mr. Berwick, "that is a fire station as well! Did you know that?"

Ellie spoke up. "We didn't know what the building was at first – but, my brother, Benjamin, noticed the word, "ENGINE" above one of the huge front doors, and then he saw 'ENGINE HOUSE NO. 6' near the top of the building, so we thought it was a fire station. We stopped by because we went to the historical society, and they are moving their headquarters to that fire station building near us. When Ellie and her brother took the assistant director's Dalmatian dog there for a walk, he started sniffing and dug up an old collar. He has been carrying that collar around with him a lot ever since!"

Mr. Berwick smiled. "Dalmatians have a great sense of smell. They have served us well as firefighter helpers for many years. Do you know anything about the collar he found?"

Mrs. Simpson smiled. "Yes, we did some research at the library and found out that we think Ryan dug up an actual *dog* collar. And, we also found out from the animal shelter that Ryan might have belonged to a firefighter from *your* fire station! This is why we came by today — to see if anyone knew anything about Ryan before he went to the animal shelter."

Just then the fire station captain, Jack Wallace, walked in. "Well, now, that's quite an interesting story! I heard a few pieces of it as I was coming in to say hello."

Captain Wallace remembered more about Ryan. "Fire stations usually don't have dogs anymore. But one of our firefighters brought his own Dalmatian to work with him sometimes and all the firefighters enjoyed having her around. One day when she was here, she had a litter of puppies. One of those pups was adopted and taken home by one of the other firefighters. But as I recall someone in the family was allergic to dogs and they couldn't keep him."

Ellie's mind was whirling again as she put the pieces of the puzzle together. "So, Ryan's mother belonged to one of the firefighters at Station 10, who brought her to work with him — and Ryan was born at Station 10! That means he has always been part of a firehouse family."

"Yes, I guess you could say that," said Mom.

Captain Wallace was glad to help and said, "Since you are so interested in Dalmatians and these historic fire stations on West Broad Street, let's go look at our history book of this building and see what we can find out!"

The captain pulled the huge, old book off the shelf.

"Look at this!" Captain Wallace pointed to the picture of Engine House No. 6, the building down the street from where the Simpsons lived.

"That's Engine House No. 6!" said Captain Wallace. "Look at those old fire engines pulled by horses! Did you know that some of the *first* fire engines were built right here in

Columbus, Ohio? The Sutphen Corporation[6] has been making fire engines since 1890 – for over 100 years!"

"Wow, that is amazing!" said Jane. "I had no idea that some of the first fire engines were built in Columbus."

"Look at how beautiful the building used to be – the fire station down the street from our house," said Ellie. "And, check out those two dogs sitting out front!"

Captain Wallace continued. "As the history book shows, those dogs in this picture of Engine House No. 6 look like they could be the parents or grandparents of the Dalmatians that have served at Columbus fire stations through the years. So, I would think that the old collar Ryan won't let go of is a collar that was worn by one of his ancestors – great-grandparents or something close to that!"

"Oh, wow!" said Jane. "This is *really* amazing!"

Ellie smiled. "Now, I know why Ryan was so excited to be digging and sniffing at the old building down the street! Maybe his ancestors lived there! It is all making sense!"

"Mom, this weekend, let's see if we can get Ryan again from Town Street and take him for another walk so he can explore Fire Station No. 6 some more. He will love it, I bet! It's the home of his ancestors!"

Ryan was so happy to see Ellie and her mom on Saturday. He was wearing his "old, new" collar that Anne was able to get repaired for him. Anne hooked his leash onto it, and he was more than ready to jump into Mrs. Simpson's car with Ellie.

As Mrs. Simpson, Ellie, and Ryan got out of the car in front of Engine House No. 6, Ellie looked up at it again. "I'm so glad the Columbus Historical Society is restoring this beautiful, old building and not tearing it down! It still has some of its old charm, don't you think, Mom?"

"It definitely does, Ellie. It will be a beautiful building when it is completed. I hate to see all the old buildings destroyed just to put up new ones. The city loses part of its history that way, I think."

"Just think, if they had torn down this building and built something new, Ryan might never have found his ancestor's collar," said Ellie.

Ryan kept pulling at the leash to explore the fire station. "Let's go!" Ellie continued. "Ryan can't wait!"

Chapter 8. Making the History Connection

Back at work, Anne told Barb and her co-workers about Ryan's collar and his connection to the old fire station. They were all so happy for Ryan. He would now get to spend some time where his Dalmatian ancestors lived!

Anne called Mrs. Simpson to let her know how much happier Ryan seemed, and Mrs. Simpson reported this news at the dinner table.

Ellie asked, "Why do you think the Columbus Historical Society chose this building, Mom?"

"Because it is in a very historical area of Columbus. Not only is it an historic property, but it is in a perfect location with the Harrison House[7] near it as well."

"What's the Harrison House?" asked Ellie.

"It's the house down the street from us at 570 West Broad Street, and it is named for William Henry Harrison," said Mom.

Ellie looked puzzled. "Who's William Henry Harrison?"

"He was our ninth United States President! Do you remember reading about 'Tippecanoe and Tyler, too?' He got the nickname, 'Old Tippecanoe' when he was in command of the U.S. Army that won the Battle of Tippecanoe in Indiana during the War of 1812. 'Tippecanoe and Tyler, too!' was the 1840 winning presidential campaign slogan for President Harrison and Vice President John Tyler. And, also, believe it or not, President Harrison's father signed The Declaration of Independence!"

"Wow — really?" said Ellie.

"Yes, really," said Mom. "I looked up some information about the Harrison House because I didn't know much about it either. What I found out is that the Harrison House was built by Colonel Robert Culbertson, a Revolutionary War veteran. When Harrison was a General in the U.S. Army, before he became President, his troops were camped here in Franklinton during the War of 1812. General Harrison may have used the Culbertson home as his headquarters."

"So, that house is right down the street from us?" asked Ellie. "Maybe we could go and see it sometime, Mom."

"Good idea, Ellie. I'll find out when it's open. It has been restored, and I think it can be used for meetings and small events. I'll call the Columbus Historical Society office[8] to get more information."

Mom continued, "This neighborhood where we live is called Franklinton. It is named after Benjamin Franklin. New settlers were encouraged to move here when there were no other cities or towns for miles. Columbus wasn't even here then. There was even one street where people were offered a free parcel of land to build a home to settle there. That's the street not far from the fire station that's called 'Gift Street.' "9

"That's so interesting, Mom!" said Ellie.

"In 1795, Lucas Sullivant came here from Virginia to survey the land that was to be given as payment for former soldiers who had fought in the Revolutionary War. He loved the area, purchased a lot of property, and founded Franklinton in 1797. The Sullivant Land Office was one of the places he used to give or sell lots in Franklinton. It was built in 1822, and it's still there. It is located behind the Harrison House."10

"Also, the Deardurff House is near us, down the street from the Harrison House on Gift Street. It was built in 1807, and it was the first post office in Columbus. It's the oldest structure in Columbus on its original foundation."11

"After all this time?" said Ellie. "It's amazing that the building is still standing!"

Mom laughed. "You are so right, Ellie! It is easy to lose sight of our connections to our own historical past. It is always good to learn about it, so we don't forget it."

Chapter 9. Lots of Changes

Soon, school let out for the summer. Benjamin and Ellie were excited to be outside and play soccer, swim, and take long walks.

Many changes were happening now at Engine House No. 6 on West Broad Street. Although the renovations were not quite finished, Anne was already working there, unpacking boxes, and preparing the new space for visitors. Ryan was thrilled to come to work with Anne at Engine House No. 6. Now, *Ryan* enjoyed taking Ellie and Benjamin for a walk instead of Ellie and Benjamin taking Ryan for a walk! Ryan loved showing them around his new "digs"!

Often, they stopped to look at the historical exhibits that Anne was putting up. They visited with the workers who were still in the process of restoring the original space. Outside, they could see how the building was initially built and how beautiful it now looked.

Also, Ryan made a new friend who came to visit as well! Once the Columbus Historical Society found out about the research into Ryan's background, Anne was able to find his sister, Ruby, who lived with another family close by. The family would bring Ruby over to join Ryan, and they got to explore the new building together. The dogs seemed to sense that the space was part of their history.

Ryan and Ruby walked Benjamin and Ellie throughout the building, and they all watched the renovations that were taking place. The workers enjoyed seeing Ryan and Ruby, petting them, and giving them treats.

There were so many interesting things to see *and* smell! They could still see the stables where the horses were kept at the fire station. The horses lived there so they could quickly pull the horse-drawn fire engines to a fire. They saw the hay loft that held the hay to feed the horses, and *even Ellie* thought she could still smell the hay! They saw where the fireman's pole was located, but they were careful not to get too close! The workers had built a temporary covering for the opening on the second floor where the pole used to be located so no one would accidentally fall through and land on the first floor of the building! Ryan and Ruby, along with Benjamin and Ellie, watched the workers sand and refinish the old floors and windows. Benjamin and Ellie were excited. The Columbus Historical Society's new home, where Ryan could visit on days he came to work with Anne, was coming along and was becoming a beautiful building once again.

Ryan's life had certainly changed. And, now, life might be bringing changes for Benjamin, Ellie, and the Simpson family.

Two weeks after school was out for Benjamin and Ellie, Dad finished his classes and earned his master's degree. The whole family attended the graduation ceremony and were very proud of Dad when he walked across the stage in his cap and gown and was presented with a beautiful diploma to certify his accomplishment.

Dad had been going on job interviews and several of the offers he was considering were from companies that would require the family to move again to another city by the time school started again in August. Although Benjamin and Ellie were happy for him, they knew they would miss their friends and their home in Franklinton.

Dad understood. "I know it's hard for you, Benjamin, and Ellie, to think about moving, especially because we have all loved living here in Columbus and learning all about the history of Franklinton."

Ellie thought about Ryan and his big change. "You know, Mom and Dad, Ryan made a difficult move that turned out to be a great change for him. So, I guess we can do it, too."

While Dad and Mom were deciding which job offer to accept and making preparations for a possible move, Dad received a call from the president of the company he had worked for before the family had come to Columbus, and it was wonderful news for the Simpson family. Since Dad had now completed his master's degree, he was offered the chance to return to his former company and would receive a promotion. In addition, the new job would be at the company's headquarters in Columbus. It was a perfect fit for the Simpsons, and, after a conversation with Mom, Dad accepted the offer. His decision to return to school for a master's degree and his successful completion of the program could not have turned out any better. The whole family had been under stress at the expectation of moving again. Now they were delighted to have the chance to stay in Columbus.

After moving to a larger house with a yard, Ellie and Benjamin adopted a big Dalmatian from the animal shelter, and they named him "Riley." Riley loved being part of a wonderful family.

When school started again in August, the family was settled into their new home. Benjamin had prepared himself for a move that would mean a new school, new friends, and a new soccer team, but was happy to return to his familiar surroundings. He loved his classes and teachers – especially his math class!

And, Ellie also enjoyed returning to her school and friends as well. From the animal shelter, she learned of another family who had adopted a Dalmatian and they became friends. Ellie's new friend, Jasmine, had named her Dalmatian "Bailey." Ellie and Jasmine often took Riley and Bailey for long walks together at Schiller Park, Goodale Park, and other beautiful historic parks in Columbus.

As for Ryan, he was very happy visiting Engine House No. 6! Anne loved having Ryan with her when she went to work, and Ryan enjoyed seeing all the visitors again. Anne even created new "paw" prints that looked like old "paw" prints that were found during the renovation process.

The firefighters from the Broad Street No. 10 fire station often came to get Ryan and Ruby so they could spend the afternoon at a real, working fire station! They got to visit with the firefighters there, where they got lots of big hugs, lots of dog treats, and lots of fun rides on the fire truck when the firefighters were not on emergency runs. Ruby proudly wore her bright red collar, and Ryan loved wearing his "old, new" collar all the time! He never took it off except when he was getting a bath.

The Columbus Historical Society wanted to recognize the important role that Dalmatians played in the early development of horse-drawn fire engines.[12] The dogs helped to clear the way ahead of the horses so the fire engines could quickly get to those who needed help. Today, the Dalmatians are no longer needed to clear the path to a fire or an emergency since the loud sirens on fire trucks now warn drivers and people to get out of their way. But Dalmatians will always be part of the history of fire stations, including Engine House No. 6.

To honor Ryan and his Dalmatian breed, the Columbus Historical Society gave Ryan a prominent place at Engine House No. 6 and an official fireman's badge! He was a happy "rescue," and he loved being with Anne at the new home of the Columbus Historical Society.

Chapter 10. Ryan's Rescue

"I can't get enough of this place!" thought Ryan. "I love all the new sights and smells! I feel like I am home again. Not sure why – but, it just feels right to me. I love sniffing and smelling and exploring the property – inside and outside."

"I can smell dog smells and other smells, especially horse and hay smells. I'm sure there were horses here sometime in the past!"

Ryan's rescue from the shelter had turned out perfectly for him. And the Columbus Historical Society's "rescue" of Engine House No.6 was turning out beautifully, too. Instead of being boarded up or torn down, it was being restored. Soon it would be the home of museum exhibits on the history of Columbus and a lively center for events, programs, and community activities. After serving Columbus for decades as a fire station, it would now serve the city as the home of the Columbus Historical Society.

"I love being here!" The feeling made Ryan smile. "I even have my sister coming to visit me with a new family down the street. Her name is Ruby, and we explore this place together. We have so much fun! And, I get to put my "paws" on lots of things these days, like cards and pictures."

"All the visitors who come in to learn about Columbus' history get to see my paw prints. And, I get my picture taken a lot these days. They have a handsome statue of me here, and people love to pat my head and get their picture taken with it! The Columbus Historical Society even gave me an official badge to recognize my "Grandpaw," and named me, 'Chief Dalmatian'! What a wonderful life!"

About the Author and Illustrator

DIANA KLINE has taught in higher education for many years, primarily in the computer science field. She holds B.S. and Ph.D. degrees from The Ohio State University and an M.S. degree from Indiana University. Also the author of *A Solar System Chat*, Diana currently resides with her husband in Columbus, Ohio.

SUZY CORNETET's artistic experience includes landscapes, portraits, structures, and scenery using water- and oil-based media. Suzy received training at the Columbus College of Art and Design as well as instruction by various professional artists. Also the illustrator for *A Solar System Chat*, Suzy and her husband are life-long residents of Columbus, Ohio.

YOUR HELP MATTERS: PLEASE CONTRIBUTE TO OUR RENOVATION OF ENGINE HOUSE NO. 6

The Columbus Historical Society's renovation of Engine House No. 6 on West Broad Street in Franklinton is far from being completed. Construction costs have more than doubled since the project began. Consequently, when our new home opens to the public later this summer, the primary exhibit and community events room will be part of the unfinished portion of the building.

The renovated fire station will be a fantastic addition to Columbus and its Franklinton neighborhood when it is completed. The primary exhibit room will serve as both an event space for local groups and a place for historical exhibits and programs. Other rooms will serve as CHS offices, host educational classes, and store historical archives, and a second-floor research library, with its large windows overlooking Broad Street and the downtown skyline, may also be available for special events.

We know that you have numerous options for your charitable donations, but would you please consider making a contribution to this important project? With your help, the renovation will ensure that Engine House No. 6 remains a vibrant hub for history, culture, and education for years to come

Making a contribution is easy. Just point your phone's camera at the QR code above and connect with our donation page at www.columbushistory.org. Or mail a contribution to Columbus Historical Society at 717 West Town Street, Columbus, Ohio 43222.

Can't afford to make a donation? You can still help the project. Volunteer opportunities are also available for interested parties. Call us at 614-224-0822.

A collage of photos from Engine House No. 6 in various stages of renovation by CHS trustee Doug Tracy. The old firehouse, which was completed in 1892, served the city of Columbus until it was taken out of service in 1966 and auctioned off in 1967.

Columbus Historical Society
717 West Town Street
Columbus, Ohio 43222
(614) 224-0822

Jack Benjamin, President
Bob Hunter, Vice-President
Adrienne J. Hostetler, Treasurer
Jodell Maclean, Secretary
Aimee Briley, Director of Operations

TRUSTEES

Chris Amatos
Grant Ames
David Maurice Bailey
Richard E. Barrett
Andrea Bogetti-Plymale
Kim Campbell
Diane Frush
Brad Funk
Erin Gibbons
Gretchen Hummel
Joyce Johnson
Kay Bea Jones
Pete Kienle
Fran Ryan
David Sewalk
Tom T. Smith
James Tootle
Doug Tracy
Bruce Warner

Ryan's Rescue
By Diana I. Kline
Illustrated by Suzy Cornetet

Bob Hunter, publications editor
James Tootle, CHS publications committee chair

Endnotes

[1] https://www.dk.com/us/book/9781465408440-the-dog-encyclopedia/

[2] https://www.dk.com/us/book/9781465408440-the-dog-encyclopedia/

[3] https://dcaf.org/dalmatian-health/hearing/

[4] https://www.lsonews.com/new-book-celebrates-dogs-collars-more/

[5] https://en.wikipedia.org/wiki/Engine_House_No._10_%28Columbus,_Ohio%29

[6] https://www.sutphen.com/history/

[7] https://www.columbushistory.org/harrisonhouseandsullivantlandoffice

[8] https://www.columbushistory.org/

[9] https://www.columbushistory.org/harrisonhouseandsullivantlandoffice

[10] https://www.columbushistory.org/harrisonhouseandsullivantlandoffice

[11] https://deardurff.com/the-deardurff-house/

[12] https://www.columbus.gov/Services/Public-Safety/Fire/About-Us/Frequently-Asked-Questions

Made in the USA
Middletown, DE
19 July 2025

10749449R00033